DATE DUE

THE BOY ON THE BEACH

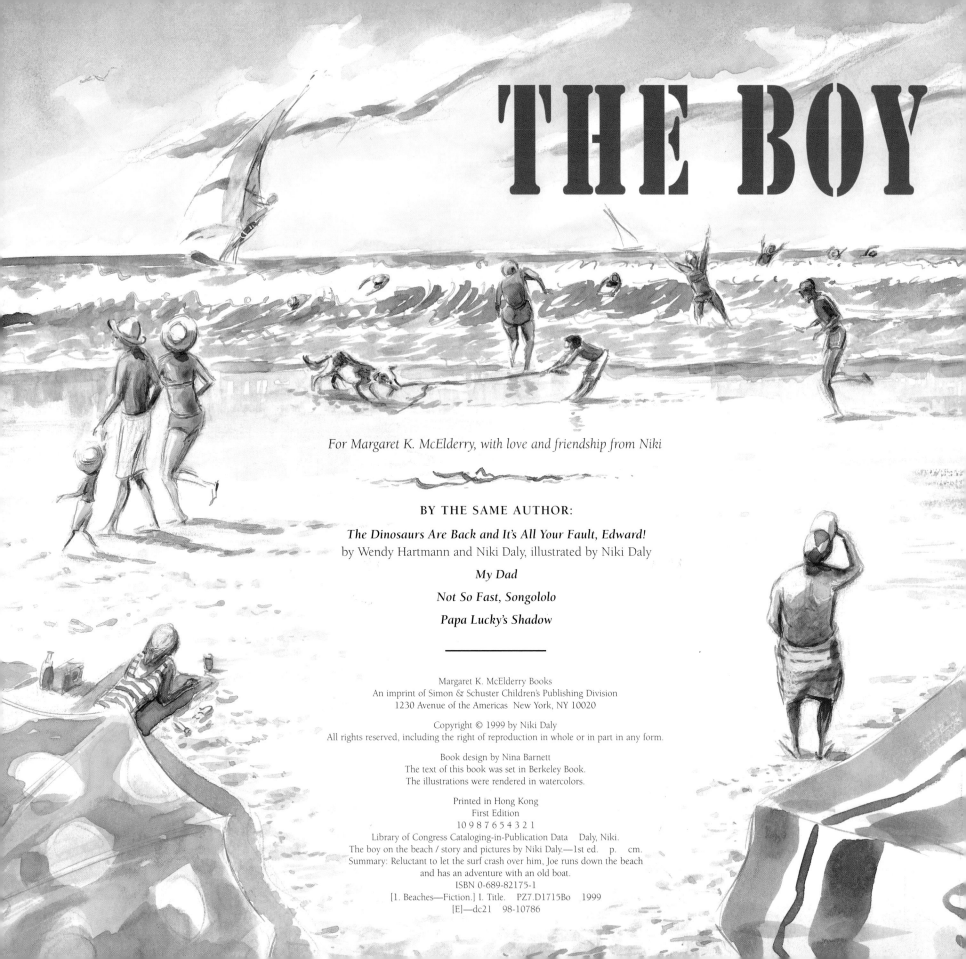

THE BOY

For Margaret K. McElderry, with love and friendship from Niki

BY THE SAME AUTHOR:

The Dinosaurs Are Back and It's All Your Fault, Edward!
by Wendy Hartmann and Niki Daly, illustrated by Niki Daly

My Dad

Not So Fast, Songololo

Papa Lucky's Shadow

Margaret K. McElderry Books
An imprint of Simon & Schuster Children's Publishing Division
1230 Avenue of the Americas New York, NY 10020

Book design by Nina Barnett
The text of this book was set in Berkeley Book.
The illustrations were rendered in watercolors.

Printed in Hong Kong
First Edition
10 9 8 7 6 5 4 3 2 1
Library of Congress Cataloging-in-Publication Data   Daly, Niki.
The boy on the beach / story and pictures by Niki Daly.—1st ed.   p.   cm.
Summary: Reluctant to let the surf crash over him, Joe runs down the beach
and has an adventure with an old boat.
ISBN 0-689-82175-1
[1. Beaches—Fiction.] I. Title.   PZ7.D1715Bo   1999
[E]—dc21   98-10786

ON THE BEACH

Story and Pictures by
Niki Daly

Margaret K. McElderry Books

It's hot, hot, hot—
hot as sun-melted tar in the beach parking lot.
"Stay close, or you'll get lost!"
calls Mom to the boy on the beach.

Between bright umbrellas and tropical towels
they find their spot.

Sandy toes . . .

sun-cream nose . . .

camera smile—*click!*

And off he goes . . .

castle-bashing,

sea-pool splashing,

surf crashing—

wet, wet, wet . . .

. . . wetting Mom, who likes to take it slow,
and Dad, who's waiting for the BIG ONE.
"Come, take my hand!" says Mom.
But the boy on the beach stands only ankle-deep
because there's just *too* much water out there.
"Come on, grab hands and you'll be all right
when the big one comes," says Dad.

SPLASH!

"Now, that wasn't too bad," says Mom.
"One more time! And I'll buy you a king-size Twister with sprinkles on top," says Dad.
But the boy on the beach says,
"NOOOO!" And off he goes . . .

leaping . . .

bumping . . .

kangaroo jumping—spraying sand wherever he goes.

SLOW DOWN!

See him zip through the crowd like a high-speed boat—
past surfers and sailboards and lazy sunbathers.
Zigzag around a smelly, shaking, shaggy dog—
but there's no time to play a wild seaweedy game.

Look there! Perched high on a dune
stands the lifeguard's lookout—
just the place on the beach for a boy to go.

And below, in a hollow, lies an old boat, waiting . . .

. . .waiting for a captain who isn't afraid of
sharks and storms and BIG ONES
that can knock a man right overboard.

Help! Help! Help!

All around, sand dunes rise like monster waves,
and the boy on the beach feels lost and alone.

Here comes the lifeguard—
as cool as a coke
and copper-tanned.
"What's up, kid?"
"I want my mom and dad,"
cries the boy on the beach.

Piggyback, over the dunes, along the crowded beach the boy goes—
all the way to Lost and Found, where his mom and dad are
waiting for him.

"There was a terrible storm. I fell out of my boat and saw a shark. The waves were EVEN BIGGER than the BIG ONE!"
"I'm glad you're safe," says Mom happily. "Now, how about that king-size Twister with sprinkles on top?" says Dad.
"Cool," says the boy on the beach, "*and* one for my lifeguard."

"My name's Bruce, but my friends call me Speedo.
What's your name, kid?" asks Speedo.
But the boy on the beach just can't stop licking.
"Tell him," says Mom. "Go on," says Dad.

A king-size Twister with sprinkles on top is *far* too yummy for a boy to talk.
So, with pointed toe in the soft wet sand, he begins to write . . .

Joe